Honey

She held everyone. Who held her?

P. A. Farrell

Book cover photo: Zaven Baghdasaryan on Unsplash.com

Amazon author page for P. A. Farrell: https://tinyurl.com/4zk9pfe6

The Pocket Companion Series contains:

When Your Mind Won't Stop

After the Loss: Finding Your Way Through Grief

You Are Enough: Rebuilding Your Self-Worth

At the Crossroads: Making Decisions When Nothing Feels Clear

When People Hurt: Navigating Difficult Relationships

When You Feel Stuck: Finding Movement in Hard Times

Books by Patricia A. Farrell, Ph.D.

When You Can't Pour From an Empty Glass: CBT Skills for Exhausted Caregivers

The Little Book on Learning Big Critical Thinking Skills

The Smart Kid's Survival Guide: Making Good Choices in a Confusing World

P. A. FARRELL

How to Be Your Own Therapist

It's Not All in Your Head: Anxiety, Depression, Mood Swings and Multiple Sclerosis

Unfiltered: Beneath the noise of our thoughts lies the true narrative of our minds

Unfiltered Again: A behind-the-scenes look at healthcare, medicine and mental health

A Social Security Disability Psychological Claims Handbook: A simple guide to understanding your SSD claim for psychological impairments and unraveling the maze of decision-making

A Social Security Disability Psychological Claims Guidebook for Children's Benefits

The Disability Accessible US Parks in All 50 States: A Comprehensive Guide

Birding in the US NOW!: A birding guide for individuals with disabilities

Contents

Chapter 1: What They Called Her

The park on Delmar Street smelled of cut grass and popcorn from the vendor who set up by the fountain every Saturday. It was early June, one of those mornings when the air still felt gentle and you could believe summer would be kind. The trees were full and green, their leaves shifting just enough to make the shade lively. Nearby, a sprinkler clicked through its rotation, sending water in a sparkling arc over grass that didn't need it but got it anyway, because that's what sprinklers do.

Ruthanne Essen pushed the stroller at a steady pace, as if she had somewhere important to go, even when she didn't. Her husband Harold walked next to her, hands in his pockets and shoulders relaxed, the way he only was on weekends. During the week, Harold was different: he got up before six, ate his toast and eggs standing at the counter, and somehow left the house with ink already on his collar. On Saturdays, he seemed more himself. He walked slowly and paid attention to the world around him.

Their oldest, a boy of seven named Dennis, ran ahead to the fountain and then doubled back, burning off energy he seemed to generate from nothing. He had the kind of legs that seven-year-old boys have in summer—perpetually scraped at the knees, always moving, belonging to no particular place for more than thirty seconds. He ran to the fountain and looked at the coins on the bottom and ran back.

Inside the stroller sat the baby.

She was eight months old and had arrived looking like she didn't quite belong to the rest of them. Dennis had Harold's dark hair and Ruthanne's square jaw. But this baby had hair so pale it was almost white, eyes as blue as a clear sky over a lake, and skin so light it seemed the sun could shine right through it. The nurses at the hospital said things like "*oh my*" and "*would you look at that*" and Ruthanne laughed each time, a little bewildered by the child she'd brought into the world.

She sat in the stroller, looking out at the world with deep, patient interest. Both her small hands gripped the railing bar, and her feet in white booties kicked in a slow, private rhythm. She watched the sprinkler, following its rotation with the focus of a scientist, her eyes tracking the arc of water each time it passed.

"Oh, my goodness."

The woman came from the direction of the rose beds, somewhere around sixty, wearing a yellow blouse and sensible shoes, the kind of woman who stopped to talk to strangers because she still believed the world was full of neighbors she just hadn't met yet. She had silver hair pinned up with the casual efficiency of someone who had been doing it that way for decades, and her face had the particular warmth of someone accustomed to finding things to like about the world. She leaned down toward the stroller with her hands on her knees, and the baby regarded her with neither fear nor excitement, just that calm, considering look.

"Look at this child," the woman said softly, the way you'd speak in church. "Just look at her." She glanced up at Ruthanne with genuine wonder on her face. "She is the most beautiful thing. She's like a little..." She laughed, searching for the word, and then she found it and smiled. "She's just a honey of a child, isn't she? What a honey."

Ruthanne laughed and said "thank you" like mothers often do, a bit embarrassed and a bit proud. Harold rocked back on his heels and grinned. The woman said a few more kind words and walked away toward the rose beds, her sensible shoes barely making a sound on the pavement.

But the word stayed.

Harold started it first, that evening at the dinner table, reaching over to wipe sweet potato from the baby's chin. "There you go, Honey." He hadn't even seemed to realize he'd said it. Ruthanne looked at him and he looked back at her, and something passed between them—that quiet, wordless language married people develop over years—and they both smiled.

Dennis tried calling her Ronnie for a few weeks, but it didn't last. Linda, who was born two years later, called her Vee for a while, but that didn't last either. Honey was the name that stayed because it was what Harold called her, and Harold's words carried weight.

Veronica Essen became Honey that Saturday in the park, and she stayed Honey for the rest of her life.

The house on Clement Avenue wasn't a large house. Three bedrooms, one bathroom, a kitchen that got too hot in August because the window faced west and the afternoon sun beat straight in through the glass. The linoleum in the hallway had a crack that ran from the bathroom door to the linen closet, and Harold had been meaning to fix it for two years running. The basement flooded every time it rained hard. The radiators in the bedrooms clanked through the night in winter, which the children had grown up with and no longer heard but which kept guests awake.

But it was theirs, or close enough that it felt like it. Ruthanne cared for it the way some women care for things they love, with a quiet, fierce attention. The curtains were always clean. The front step was swept. The woodwork around the windows was wiped down on the first Saturday of every month. The kitchen table was set for dinner every night at six, and the meal was made from whatever could be stretched the furthest. Harold's salary at the print shop was steady but not large, and there were mouths to feed, shoes to buy, and a crack in the hallway linoleum that would need fixing someday.

Honey was the third child. After her came Linda, and then the youngest, a boy named Paul, who was born when Honey was four. Paul quickly became the baby of the family, treated with a special tenderness, excused from things the others weren't, and protected a bit more from the world's roughness. He had a face that made adults want to help him, and he knew it, using it with a gentle, cheerful shamelessness.

Honey noticed this but it didn't make her bitter. If anything, it was just something she observed and filed away, the way she observed most things—quietly, carefully, without making a fuss about what she'd seen. She was that kind of child from the very beginning. While Dennis hollered and Linda chattered and Paul charmed, Honey watched. She watched the adults around her with those still blue eyes and she took in far more than anyone gave her credit for.

What she saw in those years was a family that worked. It wasn't effortless or without strain, but it was real and caring. Harold came home from the print shop with ink on his hands, sat at the head of the table, and asked each child about their day, from oldest to youngest. He listened to their answers, putting down the newspaper and paying attention. If a child's answer needed more questions, he asked them. Ruthanne made the food stretch and taste better than expected, and she never showed she was tired, even when she was. Honey could see it in the way her mother held her shoulders at the end of the evening, something tight that stayed tight, like a knot that needed to be worked out.

Honey learned a great deal from watching her mother not complain.

She learned other things too. She learned that love in a family wasn't something you said, but something you did. It was Harold getting up at five to take Dennis to hockey practice, even though the print shop started at seven and he'd be on his feet all day. It was Ruthanne sitting at the kitchen table at eleven at night, helping Linda with an essay, both of them hunched over the yellow notepad in the lamplight. Linda's handwriting got messier as she got tired, and Ruthanne's corrections grew gentler. It was the way they moved around each other in the small kitchen without bumping or needing to ask, because they knew each other's patterns so well that working together became automatic, like breathing—you don't notice it until it stops.

Honey watched all of this and understood it in a way that most children can't quite articulate. She just knew that a family was a thing you kept up, like a house—that it required tending, that you couldn't take it for granted and expect it to stay standing. She had seen what happened to the Cremmins house down the block when no one tended it: the gutters sagging, the paint going gray, the yard growing over. Families were the same. You had to show up for them every day.

She was seven years old and she already knew this.

Her father called her Honey and nothing else. Not Ronnie, which Dennis had tried for a while. Not Vee, which Linda called her sometimes. Harold Essen looked at his third child, with her platinum hair and her patient blue eyes, and he called her Honey and meant every syllable of it.

Saturday mornings belonged to them. While Ruthanne did the grocery shopping, Dennis slept in, and Linda did whatever she did on Saturdays without telling anyone. Harold and Honey had their routine. They walked to the coffee shop on Brentwood, two blocks north, past the pharmacy and the hardware store where Harold sometimes stopped to look at things he wouldn't buy. They sat in the back booth. He ordered black coffee in a heavy diner mug. She ordered hot chocolate and held it for thirty minutes, both hands around the mug, just like she once held the stroller railing in the park, as if holding on was its own kind of pleasure.

He asked her about school, about her teacher, about the books she was reading. He asked her opinion on things, real things, not the watered-down versions adults usually offered children. He asked what she thought was fair and what she thought wasn't. He asked whether she thought Dennis was being a good brother lately. He asked what she made of the news—whatever he'd been reading that week—and he listened to her answers the way he listened to things that mattered.

He asked her once whether she thought they were happy, as a family, and she had looked at him carefully before she answered.

"I think so," she said. "I think we're the regular kind of happy. Not the jumping-up-and-down kind."

Harold laughed, a real laugh that surprised him. He reached across the table and covered her small hand with his large one, the hand that always had a trace of ink in the creases no matter how well he scrubbed it, and said, "That is exactly right, Honey. That is the most right thing I've heard in a long time."

She remembered the weight of his hand, its warmth, and the gentle pressure—not squeezing, just resting there, the way he did things, without excess or show. She would remember it for the rest of her life on days when she needed to know that someone had seen her and understood exactly what she meant.

The thing about the regular kind of happy is that it is quiet enough that you can miss it while it's happening. You don't notice it the way you'd notice joy, because it doesn't announce itself. It just sits there, steady and warm, like a good furnace in the middle of a hard winter—reliable, constant, easy to ignore until you suddenly can't—and you only understand what it was worth once it's gone and the house gets cold.

The summer Honey turned twelve, she started sitting on the porch in the evenings after dinner. The street wasn't much to look at: row houses, parked cars, and the Mulroneys' dog tied to the fence three houses down, barking at everything that moved and some things that didn't. But in the summer dusk, when the heat finally faded and the streetlights came on one by one, families drifted to their porches and open windows. There was something almost beautiful about it—a whole street of people released from their indoor routines, sitting outside, just being themselves without effort.

Honey would sit on the top step with her knees pulled up and watch the street and think her private thoughts. Sometimes her father would come out and sit in the old chair by the door with the newspaper, not talking, just being there. Those were good evenings. Some of the best evenings she could remember. Two people not needing to say anything, comfortable in the same quiet.

She was growing into herself that year in a way that was slightly uncomfortable, the way growing usually is. She was taller than Linda now, which Linda resented with a cheerful openness that didn't conceal how much she actually resented it. Her hair was still pale—the platinum had softened to a color closer to honey itself, warm and faintly golden in certain light, and she'd stopped fighting it. Boys at school noticed her and she didn't know what to do about that, so she mostly ignored it, which they found more confusing than rejection would have been. She had two close friends, a girl named Joyce who wanted to be a nurse and a girl named Sally who wanted to be everything and would probably be nothing, because that was the way it went with people who wanted too much at once without being willing to choose.

She wasn't unhappy. She was a girl on the edge of something, as twelve-year-olds often are—not yet having lost the things she would eventually lose, still sure that the future was big and full and leading somewhere worth going.

She was sitting on the porch step on July fifteenth when her father came out of the house in a hurry and told her he'd be right back, just needed to run to Dawson's for cigarettes. He said it to her directly, looking at her the way you look at someone you trust to remember. His wallet was in one hand, his keys in the other, and he moved with that slight forward lean he had when he was in a rush.

"Okay," she said.

He walked down the steps and along the sidewalk with his hands in his pockets—wallet and keys both pocketed—and she watched him go the way she always watched people go, noting the details without knowing why she noted them. The set of his shoulders, which were relaxed. The slight unevenness in his walk from the knee he'd hurt years ago, an injury that had healed but not entirely. The way he raised a hand to wave at someone across the street without turning his head to see who it was, because on Clement Avenue in the summer evenings you could usually guess.

She turned back to the street. A car went past. One of the Hennessy kids rode a bicycle on the sidewalk on the opposite side. Somewhere down the block, the Mulroneys' dog barked three times and went quiet.

Her father did not come back from Dawson's.

Not that night, not walking. He made it as far as the corner of Clement and Greer, and then a heart attack took him down onto the sidewalk between one step and the next, without warning or any sign that anyone could later describe as a warning. He was there, and then he was on the ground. By the time the ambulance arrived, there was nothing left to do but confirm what the paramedics already knew.

Harold Essen was fifty-one years old. He had ink in the creases of his hands and his wallet in his pocket and the keys to the house on Clement Avenue, and he was on his way to buy a pack of cigarettes and he would have been back in ten minutes.

Honey sat on the porch step for another twenty minutes before a police car came down the street and stopped in front of the house. She watched it approach, slow down, and stop right in front, not anywhere else. She understood what it meant before either officer opened his door. She knew it the way she knew most things—not loudly or with drama, but with a terrible, certain quiet. It was the kind of knowing that happens when your body has already accepted something and is just waiting for your mind to catch up.

She was twelve years old, and the regular kind of happy was over.

She didn't go inside or ask to open the door for them. She sat on the step for the few seconds between when the officers got out of the car and when they reached the porch, and she used those seconds to finish the version of the evening where her father came back from Dawson's. She let herself have those last few seconds of the life that had existed before. Then she stood up and opened the door and let them in.

Chapter 2: What Gets Left Behind

The casseroles came first.

Nobody told you about this part. Before grief even had a name, neighbors showed up with casseroles and awkward sympathy. Ruthanne stood at the door, repeating thank you, come in, no thank you, yes, of course, while her four children drifted around the house like planets without a center.

Dennis stood in the living room doorway with his arms crossed, nineteen and freshly returned from his first year away at trade school, his face locked into something that was trying to be composed and not quite getting there. He looked, Honey thought, like he was waiting for someone to tell him what to do, and nobody was going to tell him what to do because nobody knew. Linda was fourteen and had cried so hard the first two days that she'd given herself a headache that wouldn't leave, and she sat on the couch with a cool cloth on her forehead that Ruthanne refreshed periodically. Paul was eight, and nobody was quite sure whether Paul truly understood, or whether the understanding was making its way to him slowly, the way cold water rises—you don't feel it at first and then suddenly you do and then there's no unfeeling it. Honey was twelve years old and she was the one who made coffee.

She didn't know why she started doing it. Somewhere in the blur of the first day—the police, the phone calls, Ruthanne's sister driving three hours to be there, the neighbor Mrs. Hartley crying in the hallway, her mother sitting at the kitchen table with her hands flat on the surface as if she were testing whether it was solid—Honey had found herself filling the percolator and setting it on the stove. She watched it the way her mother watched it, because that was the only instruction manual she had. She didn't drink coffee. She barely knew how to make it. She'd watched her mother do it a thousand times and she reconstructed it from memory, and when it was ready she poured it into the good cups—the ones with the blue rim that only came out for company—and brought them out to whoever needed them.

Nobody asked her to do it. She just did it because it was a thing that needed doing and nobody else was doing it.

That was, in many ways, the beginning of the rest of her life.

Harold Essen had worked at the print shop for nineteen years. He had a modest life insurance policy through his employer—modest being a word that did a great deal of work in the Essen household—and Ruthanne sat down with a woman from the insurance company three days after the funeral and came away from that meeting with a number that she wrote on a piece of paper and folded carefully and put in the kitchen drawer with the rubber bands and the twist ties. Not filed. Not put in a folder. Just tucked in the drawer where small necessities lived, as if she wasn't ready to give it the weight of something official.

Honey found the paper two weeks later when she was looking for tape. She unfolded it, looked at the number, folded it back up precisely along the original creases, and returned it to the drawer under the rubber bands. She didn't tell anyone she'd seen it.

She understood numbers. She was good at mathematics in school, better than she let most people know, because being good at math was not a quality that opened many doors for a girl in their neighborhood in 1962. But the numbers on that piece of paper told a story she could read clearly: this money would last, if they were very careful, for perhaps two years. Maybe less if something broke down or someone got sick. Maybe less if Paul needed braces, which the dentist had mentioned at his last checkup in a tone that suggested it wasn't really optional.

Ruthanne was forty-three years old and had never held a job outside the home. She had married Harold at twenty-two, had Dennis at twenty-three, and had spent the twenty years since then being exactly what she had decided to be—a mother, a wife, a keeper of the house on Clement Avenue. She was good at all of it. She was patient with children and clever with a budget and the kind of woman other women liked and trusted. None of those qualities translated directly into an income in 1962.

She found work cleaning houses.

It was not the work she would have chosen. But a woman with four children, a mortgage, and a limited set of marketable skills in 1962 did not have the luxury of choosing based on preference. She took what was available, and what was available was this: other women's houses needed cleaning, and those women would pay someone to do it. Ruthanne went to work Monday through Friday and sometimes Saturdays when someone had a special occasion coming, and she did it without complaint. She came home smelling of other people's cleaning products—a particular industrial lemon scent that Honey associated for years afterward with the sound of her mother's key in the door—and she washed her hands at the kitchen sink and started dinner, and she did not ask anyone to feel sorry for her.

Honey watched her mother work and felt something harden in her chest. Not anger, exactly. Something quieter and more determined than anger. Something that didn't have a name but that she recognized as her own version of what her mother was doing—the decision to keep going, made freshly each day, without making a production of it.

The money from the insurance policy was not enough. They all understood this by the end of the first year, though nobody said it out loud in a way that made it official, because saying a thing out loud in the Essen household was a way of making it real, and some things were easier to manage if they stayed slightly unreal.

Dennis contributed what he could from the trade school work program, which was something and not enough. Linda babysat the children two houses down, the Pearson kids, three evenings a week, and handed the money to Ruthanne without being asked, which was the most mature thing Linda had done up to that point in her life and possibly since. Honey took a job at a dry cleaner's three afternoons a week after school, pressing shirts alongside a woman named Mrs. Kessel who never said much but who taught Honey, without meaning to, that you could work with great efficiency and still keep your own thoughts entirely private. Mrs. Kessel pressed shirts and thought her thoughts and nobody knew what those thoughts were and that was the way she seemed to prefer it.

It still wasn't enough. Not quite.

The mortgage was always the problem. It was the biggest bill, and unlike groceries or shoes, it couldn't be changed or skipped. Then the furnace broke in January and used up the savings Ruthanne had set aside. Paul needed new shoes after growing three inches since September, but he didn't say anything because he knew it would be a burden. Then Linda's retainer broke—the one the orthodontist said she had to have—and replacing it cost so much that Ruthanne pressed her lips together in that way that meant she was doing the math and didn't like the answer.

Honey was in the kitchen doing homework at the table one evening in March when she heard her mother on the phone in the hallway. The house was too small for privacy to be anything but theoretical, and she could hear her mother's voice through the thin wall, not the words but the quality of the voice—the careful, deliberate steadiness of someone working hard to keep something out of her tone. Honey knew that quality. She had heard it directed at creditors, at her mother's sister when money was owed and couldn't be repaid yet, at the school when there was a question about fees.

She looked down at her algebra. She was seventeen now, a senior in high school. In fourteen months she would graduate. After graduation she had planned—had been planning since before her father died, in the vague, optimistic way of high school girls—to take a secretarial course at the community college downtown. Joyce was going to nursing school. Sally was going somewhere, she said, though the somewhere changed depending on the week.

She looked at the numbers on the page and thought about the number on the folded piece of paper in the kitchen drawer, which was long since spent. She thought about her mother's voice in the hallway. She thought about Paul's shoes, which she'd noticed because she noticed things, and about how Paul was still eight years from being on his own feet.

She did the math as she always did—clearly, without looking away from the answer, because avoiding it didn't change what was true.

She told her mother in April. She waited until Paul and Linda were out of the house and Dennis was at work, and she made two cups of tea—loose leaf, Ruthanne's preference, steeped for exactly four minutes—and put them on the table and sat down across from her mother and said, without any preliminary softening, "I'm going to leave school at the end of the year and go to work full time."

Ruthanne's face did several things in a short period of time. Honey watched all of them.

"No," her mother said. "Absolutely not."

"Mom..."

"You are not quitting school. Your father would..."

"I know what Dad would say." Honey kept her voice steady. She had practiced this talk for a month, lying awake at night, thinking through her mother's arguments and her own answers, trying to be honest without being harsh. "I also know what the numbers say."

Ruthanne was quiet. This was how Honey knew she was being heard—not when her mother agreed, but when her mother stopped objecting and went quiet instead.

"Dennis has his trade. He'll be fine in another year, maybe less. Linda has two more years and then she's done. Paul has six years, but he's young enough that things can change by the time he's ready." Honey wrapped both hands around her cup, the same way she'd always held the hot chocolate mug at the coffee shop on Brentwood, a lifetime ago. "I'm the middle. I'm the one who can step out for a while without it costing the most."

"Stepping out means not going back," her mother said. Her voice had gone flat, which was worse than if it had cracked. Flat meant she was already accepting it and hating herself for accepting it.

"Maybe. Maybe not." Honey looked at her mother steadily. "But either way, it's the right thing. And you know it's the right thing, or you wouldn't be sitting here listening to me instead of stopping me."

Ruthanne looked at her daughter for a long time. At the pale hair that had gone warmer with age, and the calm blue eyes, and the set of her jaw that was, though she'd never said it aloud, the thing about Honey's face that most resembled Harold's. The jaw that said: I've made up my mind and I'm not going to pretend otherwise.

She didn't say yes. But she didn't say no again, either, and they both understood what that meant.

Honey finished the term the way she finished everything—without dramatics, without wasted effort, getting done what needed doing. She sat her final exams and she got good grades on them, which nobody except her math teacher particularly acknowledged, and she cleared out her locker and she handed back her library books and she came home and she did not allow herself to sit with any of it for very long.

She sat in the gymnasium on graduation day and watched her classmates in their gowns and caps and thought things she didn't allow herself to think too deeply—thoughts with a shape like longing, which she recognized and set aside the way you set aside food you can't afford. Joyce was going to nursing school in September. Sally had gotten a secretarial certificate and was already talking about a job downtown, which was probably real this time. Honey was going to Hendricks Department Store five days a week starting Monday.

She folded her hands in her lap and sat up straight and looked at the stage and didn't cry.

Her mother, three rows back, cried for both of them. Honey didn't know this until Linda told her years later, because she hadn't turned around to look.

Nobody tells you that grief doesn't follow a schedule. It doesn't show up when you expect it. It can appear at seven in the morning while you're pressing shirts at the dry cleaner's, when a customer comes in and holds his collar just like Harold did—same angle, same small gesture—and suddenly you're twelve again, sitting on the porch, watching a man walk away down the sidewalk in the summer dusk. Actually, twice in the four years after her father's death. The first time was alone in the dry cleaner's back room during her break, three months after the funeral, sitting on a wooden crate behind the pressing machine where Mrs. Kessel couldn't see. She cried for about four minutes—not long, but real, the kind of crying that has weight to it—and then stopped and went back to work and pressed the rest of the afternoon's shirts and thought, in between, about her father and about the coffee shop on Brentwood and about whether the booth they always sat in had been given to someone else or whether it was still just a booth that didn't know what had happened to them.

The second time was much later, and the reasons were more complicated.

In between those two moments, she worked. She pressed shirts and then she moved to the front counter of the dry cleaner's and then, after eight months, she moved to the floor of Hendricks Department Store, where she learned to sell things to people who weren't sure they wanted them, which was a skill that turned out to be more broadly applicable than she'd anticipated. She was good with people. She was patient, which she'd learned from her mother. She was attentive, which she'd learned from Saturday mornings in a diner booth with her father. She remembered what customers told her and she used it—not manipulatively, but genuinely, in the way of someone who had simply been raised to pay attention and who found other people interesting enough to actually remember what they said.

She was seventeen when she started. She was eighteen when the floor manager noticed she was better at her job than anyone he'd hired in five years. He said this to her directly, which she appreciated, because she found honesty in either direction more useful than management.

She was still eighteen when the anxiety started.

It crept in the way those things do—not all at once but by degrees, so gradually that she almost couldn't have said when it began and would not have been able to name it as anxiety for some time. It started as a tightness in her chest on Sunday evenings when she thought about Monday, the week assembling itself in her mind in a way that felt unmanageable even when it wasn't. Then it spread to Monday mornings, and then to most mornings, and then it was simply there when she woke up before the alarm—the heart already going at a pace it had no business going, the lists already forming, the sense that things were about to go sideways combining with the knowledge that she was the only one in a position to prevent that.

She was eighteen years old and she was holding the family's finances together with her income and Dennis's contributions and her mother's cleaning money, and she had been doing this for over a year and nobody had asked her to and nobody knew the full weight of it because she hadn't told them. She hadn't told them because telling them would require someone to do something about it, and the options were limited.

The physician was a kind man named Dr. Morse who had a small practice on the same block as the dry cleaner's she'd recently left. He asked her questions in a gentle, thorough way and she answered them honestly, which was the only way she knew how to answer things. He prescribed a medication for the anxiety—a new kind, he said, quite effective, many of his patients had found it helpful—and gave her a brown prescription bottle of small white tablets and told her to take one in the morning and one if she needed it at night.

The medication worked. That was the problem with it, in the end. It worked well enough that she couldn't imagine how she'd managed without it, and then she couldn't quite remember managing without it at all, and then the morning she forgot to take it and felt the difference by ten o'clock that told her something she wasn't ready to hear.

But this was a problem she could see coming. She noticed it the way she noticed the furnace making a new noise or the crack in the linoleum getting longer. She paid attention, knowing it would need to be dealt with, and added it to the list of things that needed fixing.

For now there was work, and there was the family, and there was the mortgage, and there was Paul who still needed four more years of school before he could stand on his own feet. One thing at a time. One day at a time.

She'd learned that from her father, though he'd never put it in words. He'd just lived it, every day, in the quiet way of someone who understood that the only way through a thing was through it.

Chapter 3: The Weight of Small Things

The pills were small and white and chalky, and she kept them in the brown prescription bottle in the back of her underwear drawer where nobody would see them. This wasn't because she was ashamed, exactly. It was because she had learned, growing up in a house with thin walls and curious siblings, that the things you wanted to keep were the things you kept hidden. Not secrets, necessarily. Just private things. The distinction had always seemed important to her, though she'd never explained it to anyone.

Dr. Morse had said to take one in the morning and one at night if needed. For the first few months, she followed his instructions exactly, and the pills did what he promised. The tightness in her chest eased, her racing thoughts slowed to something she could handle, and the constant sense that something was about to go wrong faded to the background. It was like a static-filled radio suddenly coming in clear.

She could hear herself think. She could get through a Tuesday without bracing herself every hour for what might happen next.

She did her job better when she was on the tablets. She was steadier, more patient. At home, she could help Paul with his homework and talk to Linda about whatever was on her mind, all without the constant background of worry making everything harder. She hadn't realized how much energy she spent just managing her anxiety until she finally had something to help. It was like putting down a heavy bag she'd carried for so long she'd forgotten its weight.

It was around the eight-month mark that she started taking two in the morning.

She didn't decide to do it, not exactly. It wasn't a plan. One morning the single tablet felt like it wasn't reaching—the edge was still there at nine o'clock when it should have faded by eight, and the day had specific challenges in it, a difficult customer expected, a conversation with the floor manager she'd been preparing for—and she shook a second tablet out of the bottle and took it with the same glass of water and went to work without thinking too hard about it. The difference was immediate and significant. By noon she felt the way she'd hoped to feel when she'd first started: clear-headed and calm and capable of handling whatever came at her without the sense that she was doing it on borrowed time.

She told herself it was probably just a temporary adjustment. That she'd go back to the regular dose in a few days, once the week leveled out.

She didn't go back.

By the time she was twenty she was taking four tablets a day and making monthly visits to Dr. Morse to renew the prescription and sometimes, on bad stretches, stretching the bottle by cutting the tablets in half to make them last, and the days when she ran low were days she had learned to be afraid of in a specific, particular way that had nothing to do with the actual events of her life. She could be having a perfectly manageable day by any objective measure and still feel, on a low day, like the floor was slightly tilted. Like she was managing things at a one-degree slant and the effort of compensating was invisible but exhausting.

She knew this was a problem. She was not stupid and she was not without self-awareness, and the self-awareness was, in some ways, the hardest part—because she could see exactly what was happening and still couldn't stop it, which was a particularly demoralizing position to be in. She knew that the medication had become something other than what it was prescribed for. She knew she was using it to get through the day in a way that exceeded what Dr. Morse had intended. She knew that the gap between what she needed to function and what she'd needed a year ago had widened in a direction that didn't have a good explanation.

She also knew that without the medication, she couldn't do what needed to be done. The things that had to be done weren't optional, and she wasn't the kind of person to treat them as if they were. So she went to Dr. Morse each month, got her prescription, took the tablets, and handled everything else as she always did: efficiently and without making a fuss.

The department store turned out to be better than anything she'd pictured when she took the job at seventeen, though she hadn't imagined much in the first place. She took it because it was available, paid a little more than the dry cleaner's, and she needed work. She hadn't expected to be good at it in that simple way some people are—naturally, without effort, making it look easier than it was.

She could read a customer in the first thirty seconds. Not as a trick, not as a technique she'd studied—it was just the thing she'd always done with people, the same attentiveness she'd had since childhood, now in a setting where it was useful in a concrete way. She could tell what they wanted to spend versus what they'd actually brought themselves to spend, which were often different. She could tell whether they were buying something for themselves or performing a version of themselves for someone else. She could tell when a customer was in a hurry but pretending not to be, and she could tell when someone needed to take their time and would be grateful if the salesgirl let them.

She was good with the difficult customers too—the ones who came in already upset, carrying problems from somewhere else, looking for a reason to complain. She didn't take it personally and didn't force cheerfulness on them, which was usually the last thing they wanted. She stayed steady and even, the same at noon as she was at nine.

By twenty-one, she was the top seller on the floor for two months in a row. At twenty-two, she was supervising two junior staff, not because of a title but because she'd shown she knew what she was doing and people responded to that. At twenty-three, the floor manager, Gerald Finch, who wore his suits a bit too big and kept his hair perfectly parted, told her he was recommending her for an assistant buyer position.

She was twenty-three years old and she'd never finished high school.

"That won't be a problem?" she asked him.

Gerald looked at her with an expression that suggested he found the question charming in the way of things that were also a little sad. "For some stores, maybe. For me? I don't care what's on a piece of paper. I care what you can do. And I've been watching what you can do for three years."

She got the position. She learned everything it required and then a little more, because that was how she approached things. The irony of it was not lost on her—that the very situation that had forced her out of school had pushed her into a career that was making something of her in ways that school probably wouldn't have, given the options available to girls in 1964. She was practical enough to see this without resentment, though she was human enough to feel the resentment sometimes anyway, on quiet evenings when she let herself imagine the other version—the one where Harold came home from Dawson's and she graduated and went to the community college and had the ordinary, incremental life she'd been heading toward.

She imagined it and then she put it down again. Imagining things you couldn't have was a luxury she'd never been able to afford for long.

Bob Tennyson came into Hendricks on a Tuesday afternoon in March looking for a gift for his mother's birthday, which he'd waited until three days before to address. He had the look of a man who didn't buy gifts often enough to have a system—slightly overwhelmed by the options, not wanting to ask for help directly but clearly needing it. Honey approached him the way she approached most customers who had that look: without preamble, without the performed enthusiasm, with just a direct question about what he was looking for.

He told her. His mother liked scarves. She was sixty-three. She was difficult to buy for in the sense that she had opinions and wasn't shy about them.

"Then you want something she wouldn't have chosen for herself but can't argue with," Honey said.

He looked at her. "Yes. That's exactly it."

She took him to the scarf display and found the right one in about four minutes—a silk scarf in a deep teal that was unusual enough to be memorable but not so unusual as to alarm a sixty-three-year-old woman who had opinions. She could see by the way his face changed when he saw it that it was right.

She also showed him a small bottle of French perfume to go with it, because his mother sounded like a woman who would appreciate two things more than one.

He walked out with both, gift-wrapped, and he came back the following Tuesday to tell her his mother had loved it. This was unusual—customers occasionally came back to complain, but they almost never came back to report success. He told her about his mother's reaction with the particularity of someone who had been paying attention, and she found this more interesting than most things customers told her.

He asked if she wanted to have dinner.

He was twenty-seven, six years older than her, with brown hair worn slightly too long for advertising—his profession, he told her—and a way of talking with his hands that she found either endearing or exhausting depending on what he was explaining. He was smart in the confident way of people who'd been educated at good schools, which was to say the confidence sometimes preceded the thought rather than following from it. But he was also kind. She could see that. She was good at seeing it.

They had dinner and then they had dinner again and then they had dinner most Friday evenings through the spring. He met her family and was thoughtful with each of them in ways that were specific to who they were rather than generically charming, which told her something. He met Dennis and took him seriously. He met Paul and didn't talk down to him, which was the correct response to Paul. He met Linda and survived Linda's questions, which were direct and not entirely polite, which was also the correct response to Linda.

He told her he loved her in August, on the back porch of the house on Clement Avenue. He said it with his hands still for once, looking at her directly.

"I know," she said.

He blinked. "That's all?"

"I know because you show it. I've known for a while."

"But you haven't..."

"No," she agreed. "I haven't."

He was quiet for a moment, turning this over. "Can I ask why?"

She looked at the street. Someone's television was going through an open window down the block, a laugh track from something she couldn't identify floating out into the evening. "Because loving you and being able to act on it aren't the same thing right now. Paul has three more years of school. Linda's just getting settled. My mother manages, but she relies on things being steady, and they're only steady because of how they're arranged." She paused. "If I rearrange them right now, the steadiness goes."

"Your mother is a capable adult," Bob said carefully.

"She is. She's also the reason this family is still standing, and so am I, and those two things working together is what makes it work." Honey looked at him. "I'm asking you to wait. I'm not asking you to like it. I know it isn't fair."

He held her gaze for a long moment.

"So I wait," he said.

"I'm asking you to wait," she said again, which was a different thing.

He did both: waited, and didn't always like it, and kept showing up on Friday evenings anyway.

The medication problem got worse before she addressed it. That was the nature of those things—they got worse on the same slow gradient by which they arrived, unremarkable increment by unremarkable increment, until the distance between where you'd started and where you were was large enough to see clearly but had been arrived at in steps too small to have triggered the alarm at any individual moment.

It was Linda who noticed first. Linda, who had been the one Honey had spent years helping, who had been the one with the headaches and the homework and the questions and the immediate needs—Linda came into Honey's room on a Saturday morning when Honey was still in bed, which was unusual enough to be noticeable.

Linda sat on the edge of the mattress with the directness she'd had since she was a teenager and said, "You don't look right."

Honey was three days into a stretch where the refill wasn't due and she'd been cutting the tablets in quarters, and the world had taken on a gray, muffled quality that she'd been managing by sleeping more than usual and pushing through the rest. "I'm fine," she said.

"You've said you're fine for a month. And every week you look worse than the week before." Linda looked at her steadily. She had learned, somewhere in her twenties, to look at things she didn't want to look at. Honey had taught her that, mostly by example. "What is it?"

Honey looked at her sister. She weighed the options the way she weighed most things—quickly, honestly, without pretending the answer was different from what it was. And then she did what she almost never did.

She told the truth.

It came out in pieces, without drama, the way Honey did most things. The medication. How it had started, and how it had seemed like a reasonable solution to a real problem. What it had become over two years and some months, slowly and without any single moment she could point to as the turning. The refills, the calculations, the cutting, the gray days when she could feel the absence of it like something had been removed from the air.

Linda sat and listened all the way through without interrupting. When Honey finished, she was quiet for a moment that stretched long enough to be meaningful.

"You've been carrying this while carrying everything else," Linda said.

"Yes."

"And you didn't tell anyone."

"No."

Linda looked at her hands, pressed together in her lap, then looked back up. "What do you need?"

Honey had been approaching this question carefully for weeks, in the way you approach a thing you know you have to deal with but haven't yet found the nerve for. "I need a different doctor. Someone who knows more about stopping—about doing it properly, not just running out and suffering through it." She paused. "And I need you not to tell Mom."

Linda agreed to both. She went with Honey to Dr. Albright at the clinic on the west side, a woman in her fifties who had seen this particular landscape many times and who treated Honey without the faint undercurrent of surprise that Honey had half-expected—without the sense that she should have known better. Dr. Albright was matter-of-fact about it. Here was a problem, here was a way through it, here were the things that would be hard and here was why and here was what to do about each one.

Linda sat in the waiting room for the two hours Honey was inside. She brought a magazine she didn't read.

The process of stopping was slow and managed and difficult in a way that Honey would later find very hard to explain because the difficulty was not dramatic. There were no crises, no scenes, nothing that made a compelling story when she tried to tell it. It was just gray and grinding and relentless, lasting several months, and she went to work and she functioned and she managed, and she reported to Dr. Albright every two weeks and told her accurately and completely how things stood.

Eventually the gray lifted. It lifted gradually, the way good things always happened—not a moment but a direction, not a door opening but a slow brightening, until one morning she woke up and the world was the size it was supposed to be again. Not solved. Not fixed. Just the actual size, which was manageable.

She was twenty-four. The anxiety was still there under everything, the way it had always been. But it was hers now, in the sense of being something she lived with on its own terms rather than something she'd been trying to outrun. She managed it. She learned its patterns. She got better at recognizing what made it worse and what made it quieter.

She had learned something in those months that she would carry for the rest of her life: that the thing you are most afraid will destroy you, if you turn and face it squarely instead of running, is almost always survivable. Not comfortable. Not easy. Survivable. And there is a particular kind of knowledge that comes from surviving a thing you were afraid of—a knowledge that doesn't announce itself and doesn't make you braver in any showy way, but that sits somewhere underneath everything else like a second floor under the first one, holding the weight.

She filed this away with the other things she knew and didn't talk about, and she went back to her life, which was waiting for her, as it always was.

Chapter 4: How Families Work

The house on Clement Avenue had its own winter smell. Coal dust, pot roast, and the lavender sachets Ruthanne kept in the linen closet mixed with the faint dampness of old plaster and the softening wood floors, worn by years of water and weather. It wasn't a beautiful smell, but it belonged only to this house, and Honey had breathed it in for so long that she stopped noticing it, the way you stop noticing your own heartbeat. She only realized it was missing when she was somewhere else. Joyce's parents' house, for example, smelled different—just ordinary in another way—and every time she noticed, it reminded her how unique a home's smell could be, how much of the people who lived there seemed to linger in the air.

She was twenty-five that winter, the same year Paul started his last year of high school. She had worked at Hendricks for eight years, starting out pressing shirts and slowly building a career she hadn't planned but managed carefully. Now she was an assistant buyer, with her own small office, a phone extension, and responsibilities that meant she had to learn skills like negotiation, inventory planning, and spotting what customers wanted before they did. She was good at all of it. Her salary wasn't what it would have been if she were a man doing the same job. She knew this, and she had learned to accept it, filing it away with all the other unfair things she had faced—recognized, noted, but never allowed to stop her.

Bob had been waiting for six years.

He had been, in that time, patient in the way of a person who has examined his options and concluded that patience is the only strategy that has any chance of working, and has committed to it—genuinely committed to it, not with a gritted-teeth suppressed resentment but with the actual decision to be in it for however long it took. There were conversations, not arguments but conversations with weight, when he sat across from her and laid out his position clearly and she heard it clearly and they looked at each other and both understood that nothing was going to change yet. He didn't like it. He never pretended to like it. But he understood it, and understanding a thing and liking it were not the same requirement.

He had not stopped coming to Friday dinners. He had not stopped calling on the other evenings, the mid-week calls that were not about anything in particular and that she had come to rely on without quite acknowledging that she relied on them—the sound of his voice on the other end of the telephone at nine o'clock on a Tuesday being a kind of steadiness she had not sought and had found anyway. He understood that a woman who had spent a decade being the person everyone else depended on needed, above all, someone she could depend on without having to ask for it. He couldn't give her everything. He could give her that.

She never asked for it outright. But she depended on it, and he knew she did. In its quiet way, that was a promise between them.

Linda got married that spring. Her husband, Russell Kaminsky, sold insurance on the south side and had a laugh so loud it could be heard three houses away—the kind of laugh that made everyone turn. Honey liked him right away, fully and without hesitation, which was rare for her. She was kind to most people out of habit, but truly cared for only a few. That was maybe the truest thing about her: her warmth was real, but the deeper kind was rare and had to be earned.

Russell earned her trust by being exactly who he seemed. He was straightforward and genuine. He loved Linda with a mix of humor and steadiness that she needed, which wasn't easy to find. He seemed to do this naturally, which was the best part.

The wedding was small. Linda had wanted something larger—she had been planning the dress since she was fourteen, and the dress in her head had a cathedral train—and Russell's mother had opinions about the venue, and eventually, in the way of these negotiations, everyone gave up a portion of what they'd wanted and assembled something that was mostly right. The reception was held in the basement of St. Michael's with a buffet that Ruthanne had contributed significantly to, and the dance floor was linoleum that someone had waxed too enthusiastically and which was consequently quite slippery, and two of the older guests slipped and caught themselves and laughed about it and this was the story everyone told about the reception afterward.

Ruthanne cried through the ceremony and most of the dinner. She wasn't sad; it was the feeling of a mother seeing her children find a safe place. She cried quietly and fully, like someone who had earned the right to feel that way and knew it.

Honey danced once with Bob, once with Paul, and once with Dennis. The dance with Paul was the one she remembered most. He was seventeen and shy about dancing in front of others, but he agreed because Honey quietly asked him during dinner, and he never could say no to her. They both knew this, even if they never talked about it. Paul took dancing seriously—he tried hard, even when he missed a step, which made him better than Dennis, who was so relaxed he barely danced at all.

"You're better at this than you think," she told Paul.

He gave her the look he gave her when she said things he suspected were kind rather than accurate. "I'm terrible at this."

"You're committed to it. That's most of it."

He considered this. Then: "You should be allowed to be happy too, you know."

She looked at him. He was looking at the dance floor rather than at her, seventeen-year-old composure requiring that he not fully see what he'd just said.

"I know," she said.

"Paul's graduation's not that far."

"I know that too."

He finally looked at her. His face had the shape of their father's—the jaw and forehead—but his expression was his own, more direct than Harold's and less likely to leave things unspoken. "Don't wait too long after," he said. "That's all I'm saying."

She looked at him for a long time and then she squeezed his hand and they kept dancing.

At the end of the evening, waiting for their coats in the church vestibule, Bob stood beside her and said quietly, "You organized this, didn't you?"

"Linda planned it."

"Linda planned it. And by nine o'clock you'd quietly redirected about six different things that were going sideways."

She looked at him. He wasn't criticizing. His voice had that certain tone it took on when he was trying to say something he hadn't found the right words for yet.

"I see you," he said. "I just want you to know that. Not what you do. You."

She looked away, out the vestibule window at the parking lot and the cold April night. "People see me," she said.

"They see what you do," he said. "That's not the same thing."

She didn't answer. But on the way to the car, she took his arm, something she didn't always do. He didn't draw attention to it, which was exactly right.

Dennis bought a house the year after Linda's wedding. It was a small brick two-bedroom in the same neighborhood where he'd rented since trade school. He bought it because his fiancée, Gail, who worked in hospital billing and was the most practical person Honey knew, told him she wouldn't keep renting forever. Dennis listened and bought the house.

Honey visited the house on a Saturday afternoon in April, on one of those early spring days when the sky kept changing. She stood in the small kitchen with its low ceiling and west-facing window, which she thought was the wrong direction for morning light. She looked out at the yard, where a crabapple tree in the corner was just starting to bud, its branches mostly bare but showing signs of new growth.

"It's good," she told Dennis.

He was watching her from the doorway with the particular expression he'd developed in his late twenties, something more careful than he'd been as a young man. Dennis had been a good-hearted but inattentive boy who had grown into a more attentive man by the slow route of making enough mistakes to finally start noticing the cost of them.

"You okay?" he said.

"I'm always okay."

"I know." He leaned against the door frame. "That's not what I asked."

She looked at the crabapple tree. "I'm glad you're here. This neighborhood, this house." She paused. "I'm glad you're close."

"Paul's almost done," Dennis said.

"Eight more months."

"Gail thinks you should've gotten yourself set up years ago." He said this carefully, in the tone of someone delivering a message he agrees with but knows might not land well.

"Gail's probably right."

"She usually is. That's either the best or the worst thing about her, depending on the day." He pushed off the doorframe and looked at his sister—really looked at her, something he had learned to do on purpose. "I know I wasn't as present as I could have been. After Dad. I was young and I was..." He stopped. "I left you with a lot."

"You were nineteen."

"Still."

She looked at him. He wasn't asking for forgiveness—he was just stating the truth, which was different. "You're making up for it," she said. "You're here now. That's what matters."

He nodded. After a moment he said, "He knows what you've done, you know. Paul. More than you think he does."

"He said something at Linda's wedding."

"He says things. He just doesn't say them where you can hear them." Dennis smiled briefly. "He's a lot like you, that way."

She thought about that on the drive home, the city moving past the window in the particular flat light of early spring. She thought about what it meant to be known by the people you loved, and whether being known was the same as being seen, and whether either one was the same as being understood.

Ruthanne had a saying she'd brought from her own mother, who had it from hers: a family is not a thing that happens to you; it is a thing you make, every day, with your hands.

Honey had heard this her entire life. She had understood it intellectually since she was very young. She had not understood it in the way you understand a thing that has been tested until her father walked away down Clement Avenue and didn't come back. Until she made coffee for a room full of grieving people because someone had to. Until she found the number on the piece of paper in the kitchen drawer and understood what it said and started doing the math.

Now, at twenty-five, watching her siblings settle into their lives—Dennis in his brick house with Gail, Linda with Russell and his big laugh—she understood it in the way you understand something that has cost you. Not differently, just more deeply.

A family is a thing you make with your hands.

She had made this one. Not alone—Ruthanne had made it too, and Dennis in his way, and Linda when it mattered most, and Paul who had grown up watching all of it and absorbed more of it than any of them had realized. But there was a version of the Essen family of Clement Avenue that would not have held together without the specific, sustained, mostly invisible effort of this one person. Who had given up her senior year and her graduation and her college plans and a decade of Fridays and the freedom to want things for herself without immediately calculating what the wanting would cost everyone else.

She did all of it without keeping score. Or maybe she kept score privately, the way she kept most things to herself, in a place she rarely let anyone see. Still, she chose, again and again, to keep going.

She wouldn't have called it a sacrifice, at least not in the dramatic way people usually mean. It was simply the shape her life took, what she had done and who she was. She couldn't imagine doing it differently, because it felt so much like her.

But at twenty-five, with Paul in his last year of high school, there were some evenings—quiet Thursdays when the house was hers for a few hours and the week's work was done—when she let herself wonder what it would be like to be known the way Bob described. Not for what she did, but just for who she was.

She was still wondering the evening Paul graduated the following June.

She was still wondering the evening Bob took both her hands across the table at the Italian place on Hennepin and said, very quietly, "I'm done waiting for you to tell me it's time. So I'm asking. Is it time, Honey?"

She looked at him for a long time. She looked at his face, which she had been looking at for six years—the face she'd chosen to trust when she hadn't had much left over for trusting things—and she thought about her father in the coffee shop, both hands around a mug, asking her what she thought about things and meaning it.

"Yes," she said.

He let out a breath that showed her just how much the waiting had cost him. She felt a complicated tenderness for him, one she would spend years learning to understand. She thought about the ordinary kind of happiness. Maybe it was still possible. Maybe that was what was sitting across from her, asking if it was time.

She thought it probably was.

Chapter 5: Becoming Mrs. Tennyson

The wedding was in October.

It wasn't a Saturday, but a Friday evening. That had always been their day, ever since their first dinner at the Italian place on Hennepin. Neither of them had said it out loud, but both understood it. Honey picked Friday on purpose, because she liked to put meaning into small things without drawing attention to it. The meaning was there, whether anyone noticed or not.

The church was the one on Clement and Vine she'd attended since childhood, the solid brick building with the choir that had always been better than the neighborhood could reasonably expect. She had sat in the pew third from the front on the left side for thirty years—first between her parents, then beside her siblings, then alone after Harold was gone, then with various configurations of the family as they'd grown and scattered and regathered. She had wept in that building and been calm in it and thought her private thoughts in it and it felt right to marry there. Some things deserved to happen in the place where you had already learned what things cost.

The flowers were chrysanthemums in autumn colors, burnt orange and deep yellow, because her mother's garden still had them. She didn't want to spend money on imported flowers that would look like every other wedding. The ring on her left hand still felt new. She had worn so few things on her hands over the years—no rings, no bracelets, just the watch her mother gave her at twenty-one. Now, she noticed the weight of the ring every time she looked down.

Ruthanne walked her down the aisle.

Some guests raised an eyebrow, having their own opinions about how things should be done. Dennis had offered, genuinely and without awkwardness, showing how much he'd grown. She thanked him and said no. She thought carefully about who the right person was, and what 'right' meant in this case, but she already knew the answer. The right person was the one who had stood by her through everything. The one who cried on graduation day for both of them. The one who sat across from her in a kitchen in April and said: I'm not going to stop you. Not yes, just not stopping her, which was exactly what Honey needed.

That was her mother.

Ruthanne wore a dress in a dove gray that Honey had helped her pick out over three Saturday afternoons of shopping that had been, in their own way, the most pleasant three Saturdays Honey could remember in recent years. Just the two of them moving through stores with the focused attention of women who know what they are looking for and are not going to be distracted by things that are merely pretty. They found the right dress on the third Saturday, and Ruthanne had stood in the fitting room mirror and said, "Well. That'll do," which was Ruthanne for: this is exactly right.

She walked her daughter down the aisle with the straight back and the lifted chin of a woman who understands the weight of what she's carrying and is not going to let it show except in the brightness of her eyes, which was showing a great deal. Honey watched the floor for the first part of the walk and then made herself look up, made herself look at Bob at the end of the aisle, and she saw his face from that distance and she kept walking.

They used the standard vows from the church. Honey had tried twice to write her own, but put the paper away both times. It wasn't that she couldn't find the words, but she didn't feel the need to say them in front of everyone. Her feelings were private. She would show them over time, in her own way—by being present, by being reliable, by giving steady attention that builds into something the other person can depend on.

She stood at the altar and watched Bob's face as she spoke the standard words. His expression was one she had seen only a few times before—completely unguarded, with all his usual careful polish gone. He looked at her the way her father once looked at her mother in the kitchen on Clement Avenue, long ago. It was the look of someone who has decided this is the most important thing in the room and wants it to stay that way. He wasn't performing. He was simply being.

In that moment, she let herself believe it. She accepted it the way you accept something you've been offered but never let yourself want. She was thirty-one, and for half her life she had given herself to other people's needs. Now, someone was offering something back. She stood at the altar and opened her hands.

They found a house in a neighborhood twenty minutes from Clement Avenue. It was far enough to be their own place, but close enough that Honey could get there quickly if she needed to. She never said this out loud—it was just the distance she felt comfortable with, and Bob understood without being told. Over the years, he was getting better at understanding the things she didn't say. He wasn't perfect, but he tried in the way that mattered: he tried consistently.

The house was a brick colonial with three bedrooms, a yard that backed onto an alley, and a kitchen with a window facing east. The morning light coming through that window was what made her choose it. She stood in the kitchen at ten in the morning during the viewing and watched the light on the linoleum. It was direct and warm, falling across the counters in a way that made the room feel full of possibility, not just adequate. She thought: this is a kitchen where things get done. This is a kitchen I can work in.

She had spent her entire life in kitchens that faced west. This was the first one that would give her the morning.

They moved in on a gray Saturday in November with help from Dennis and Russell and Paul, all three of whom had the particular male competence of men who have moved things before and have strong opinions about the right way to do it. The boxes went in efficiently if not always where Honey had planned, and Bob directed traffic and tried to be helpful and mostly was. Ruthanne arrived midway through with a pot of soup and left it on the stove with a handwritten note about reheating and departed without ceremony, because she understood that her presence was a gift that worked best in the right measure.

That night, after everyone had left and the boxes were stacked and the furniture was roughly in place, Bob opened a bottle of wine and sat on the kitchen floor with his back against the lower cabinets, since there was nowhere else to sit yet. Honey sat beside him. They passed the bottle back and forth and didn't talk much. The house made small sounds, like a place still getting used to its new owners: the radiator finding its rhythm, the windows settling in the wind.

"Happy?" he said.

She looked at the east-facing window, dark now, just the streetlight making the raindrops on the glass into small bright points.

"Yes," she said. "The regular kind."

He smiled, not knowing what she meant, and she put her head on his shoulder, and that was the first night in the house that would be hers for the next fifty years.

Her mother came to Sunday dinners. This wasn't something they formally arranged—there was no conversation where they agreed it would happen—but it became the pattern within the first month. Patterns, once set, often become more reliable than agreements. Ruthanne arrived at one o'clock with something she'd made: a cake, a jar of pickled beets from her summer canning, or sometimes a pot of chili because Bob had mentioned three Sundays earlier that he liked it. Ruthanne remembered everything anyone told her that might be useful later.

She sat at the kitchen table and talked to Honey while Honey cooked, and the conversation between them in those years had the quality that comes to mothers and daughters who have done the hard work of earning each other's respect: honest without being harsh, easy without being shallow, candid in proportion to the subject at hand. They disagreed about certain things, as people who see the world from different vantage points will, and the disagreements were clean—said and responded to and set down, not carried forward into the following week.

Ruthanne had opinions about Bob that she largely kept to herself, which Honey appreciated. What she offered instead was consistent warmth toward him and genuine interest in the things he cared about, and Bob, who had grown up in a household where warmth was expressed more formally, was charmed by this in the way of someone who has been hungry for something without knowing the name of the thing.

"Your mother," he said one Sunday evening after Ruthanne had gone, while Honey was finishing the dishes. "Is the most quietly intelligent person I think I've ever met."

"I know," Honey said.

"She listens to everything and forgets nothing."

"I know that, too."

He was quiet for a moment. "You're exactly like her."

She turned to look at him over her shoulder, and something in her expression made him add quickly, "That is the highest compliment I know how to give."

She turned back to the dishes. "Good," she said.

The children came. Carol was born in 1971, with her father's dark hair and her mother's thoughtful eyes. She was a baby who studied the world from the start, with a seriousness the pediatrician found unusual but Honey found familiar. James arrived in 1973, loud from the first day, always sharing his opinions and only changing them when given strong reasons. Thomas was born in 1976, the quiet one, who listened before he spoke and still did this at forty-five.

Honey went back to Hendricks after each of them. Four months after Carol, three after James, four after Thomas, because the fourth time was harder and she was honest with herself about what she needed. She arranged for Mrs. Gruber—a woman of sixty with efficient hands and a genuine affection for children that she expressed through competence rather than coddling—to come in three days a week, and she managed the rest with the organizational efficiency of someone who had been managing complex logistics since she was seventeen and had never fully stopped.

Bob was a present father in the ways that mattered to him: the school events, the baseball coaching, the knowing of names and asking of specific questions. He was better at this than many of the men he worked alongside, who left more of the parenting to their wives without appearing to notice that they were doing so. Honey gave him credit for this without totaling up the rest of it—the things that weren't being done, the calculations she was making constantly that he wasn't part of.

What she didn't do was ask. This was her tendency—the preference for doing over asking, the deep reluctance to name a need and thereby make it visible and therefore someone else's burden. She ran the household because she ran it, because she was better at it and more attentive to it, and because the machinery of it was already in her hands and it was easier to keep it there than to explain it to someone else.

She kept track of who needed what. She signed permission slips the day they came home, not the day before they were due. She remembered that Carol couldn't eat strawberries, that James had a math test every other Friday, and that Thomas needed fifteen minutes of quiet after school before he was ready to talk. She managed all this along with her job at Hendricks, where she was now a full buyer with her own department and a reputation among vendors for being fair, exact, and not easily swayed by charm.

She liked the work. She always had. Work made things clear in a way most other things didn't. It had concrete requirements and measurable outcomes, letting her use her organizational skills to create visible results by the end of the day.

And she became, without any ceremony or announcement, the matriarch.

She wasn't just the matriarch of her own household. She was the matriarch for all of them—Clement Avenue, Linda's house, Dennis's house, Paul's apartment, and eventually Paul's house in another city. She was the one they called. She was the one who showed up. She kept the whole family's picture in her head: Dennis's oldest and the nut allergy, Carol's fear of dogs from a bad moment at age four, James's trouble with certain teachers, and what Paul's ex-girlfriend had done and why it mattered. She held things—quietly, without calling attention to the holding, without expecting to be thanked for it, and without entirely knowing, from day to day, how much of herself it was consuming.

But it was weight. Whether anyone named it that or not, it was weight.

Chapter 6: The Ring

She found out on a Wednesday.

It wasn't lipstick on a collar or a strange number on a phone bill. Those belonged to other marriages, other decades, other women who might have watched for signs in a way Honey never did. Watching for signs wasn't the same as trusting, and she had chosen to trust. She found out because she answered a call on their home phone meant for Bob, and the woman on the other end said hello with a kind of familiarity that told Honey, in the first word, everything she needed to know.

The woman's voice wasn't flirtatious. There was nothing Honey could point to as proof. It was just familiar, the way a voice becomes when it knows someone in a way it shouldn't. There was an ease there, something that had been earned.

The woman asked for Robert.

No one in Bob's life called him Robert. Not his mother. His colleagues at the firm called him Bob or Tennyson, but never Robert. Only someone who used his full name as a way to set him apart, to have her own word for him, different from everyone else's.

Honey said, very evenly, "I'm sorry, he's not home. Can I take a message?"

There was a pause on the other end. It wasn't quite surprise. It was more like recalibration.

"No," the woman said. "Thank you."

The line went dead.

Honey held the receiver for a moment, feeling the plastic in her hand, the weight of it. She set it back in the cradle carefully, the way she always set down things that mattered. She stood in the kitchen. The late afternoon light came through the east-facing window just as she had loved since the day they saw the house. It was low and golden, falling across the counter and lighting up the ordinary things: the mail, the coffee cup Bob left in the sink that still needed rinsing, the pad of paper for the week's grocery list.

She stood in that light for a while and thought about what she knew, which was a great deal, and what she was going to do with it, which she did not yet know.

The children would be home in an hour. Carol was seventeen and had her own life now, the way seventeen-year-olds do—present in the house but mostly elsewhere in her attention. James was fifteen and in the middle of a difficult stretch, the kind boys had when they were finding the edge of everything and testing it. Thomas was twelve and still, some evenings, the child she recognized most clearly—the one who would come and sit near her without asking for anything in particular, just for the proximity.

She stood in the kitchen until the light shifted, and then she started dinner.

She didn't confront Bob that night. She wasn't someone who acted on her first surge of feeling, not because she couldn't feel, but because she understood something she had known since she was twelve years old, sitting on a porch step. The first surge was almost never the whole truth. It was just the shock, and shock was not the same as understanding. She needed to understand before she acted, because acting without understanding often made things worse.

She waited four days. She went about them as she always went about her days—feeding the children and going to work and managing the house and talking to her mother on the phone Wednesday evening about her mother's garden, which had produced an exceptional crop of tomatoes that year. She listened to her mother talk about the tomatoes and she asked the right questions and she was present in the conversation, because her mother deserved her full presence and Honey had been giving people her full presence for long enough that she could do it even when a part of her was occupied elsewhere.

Underneath all of that, the part of her that was always working kept doing its job. It examined the problem from every angle, stayed honest about what she found, and refused to look away from what she saw.

She thought about the house with the east-facing kitchen window. She thought about Sunday dinners with her mother.

She thought about what it meant for the family. The family that she had been building for twenty years, since before she had her own family, since she was seventeen pressing shirts and making coffee for grieving people and doing the math on a folded piece of paper.

The family. Always the family. And she was clear-eyed enough, sitting with this for four days, to know that the family was not an excuse. It was a real reason. A real consideration. She was not staying out of fear or pride or inability to imagine another life. She was staying because the destruction of this household would cause damage to three specific people who didn't deserve to absorb that damage, and she was the person in a position to prevent it.

This was her choice. She made it with her eyes open.

On the fourth evening she came downstairs after the children had gone to their rooms and found Bob at the kitchen table with a scotch poured and not yet touched, which told her that he had been sitting there waiting and was aware she was coming. The untouched drink was its own kind of admission—he hadn't needed it, he'd just needed to be holding something.

She sat down across from him and put her hands flat on the table. She hadn't meant to copy her mother, but she had made this gesture at moments of reckoning since she was twelve.

"How long," she said.

He looked at the glass. "Eight months."

She took this in. Eight months was not a short time. It wasn't a single mistake that was quickly regretted. Eight months had its own shape and history. She sat with this for a moment, then let it go.

"Is it over?"

He still wasn't looking at her. "It can be."

"That is not the same thing."

He looked up then. "No," he said. "It isn't. I know it isn't."

She looked at him for a long time. She had always been good at facing things directly, even as a child, and she looked at him now with all she had. She saw the guilt on his face, which was real, and the relief underneath it, which was also real. It was the relief of being known. She understood this. She had spent her life carrying things alone and knew the exhaustion of it, and the weight that lifts when someone finally shares what you know.

She also saw, beneath both of those feelings, what had always been there: he loved her. That was never in doubt. In some ways, that was the hardest part of the evening, because a love that could exist alongside this kind of carelessness was more complicated than the love she thought she had. It was real, but it wasn't enough, and both things were true at once. She would have to find a way to live with that.

"I'm not leaving," she said.

Something moved across his face: relief, and beneath that, a complicated guilt about feeling relieved.

"The children need their father at home and present. They don't need to know what this is, and I am not going to dismantle what I've spent twenty years building because you weren't careful enough with it." She paused. "That's not who I am. It was not who I was when I agreed to marry you and it's not who I am now."

He nodded. His eyes were wet. She noticed this without being moved by it in the way she might once have been moved—the witness to his pain was different now from how it had been, and she recognized this with a sadness that was clean and specific.

"But things are not the same," she said. "You understand that."

"Yes."

"And they will not look the same. I want you to understand what I mean."

He waited.

She reached down to her left hand and worked the wedding ring off her finger. The ring she had worn for all those years, the ring that had been on her hand through all three children and all the Sunday dinners and all the Friday nights and the ordinary days that had made up the life they'd made together. She set it on the table between them—not slammed, not thrown, nothing theatrical—just placed it there, on the wood, between their two hands, and then she stood up.

"I'm going to bed," she said. "The children have school tomorrow."

She did not wear the ring again.

This was noticed by everyone and remarked on by almost no one, because the quality of attention Honey gave to everything she did communicated, clearly and without requiring explanation, that this was a decision and not an oversight. A woman who pressed her clothes carefully and kept a tidy house and remembered every appointment did not simply forget to put on her wedding ring. The absence was a statement, and the people who knew her well enough to read it read it correctly.

Her mother noticed at the first Sunday dinner after. She looked at Honey's hand when Honey set the serving dish on the table, and then she looked at Honey's face, and she said nothing, which was exactly the right response and exactly what Honey had known she would do.

Linda noticed and called on a Monday morning. "I don't need to know what happened," she said. "I just want you to know I'm here."

"I know," Honey said. "Thank you."

"Is there anything..."

"No. But thank you for asking."

Linda had learned, over the years, to receive this kind of answer from Honey without pushing, because pushing Honey when she'd drawn a line only moved the line further back. She let it go and they talked about other things, and the call ended on the ordinary note it had started on, and this was itself a gift—the gift of being treated normally when everything wasn't normal.

The children were old enough to notice the missing ring, but young enough to need the household to stay together. So the ring was gone, nothing was said, and the days kept their usual shape. Dinner at six. School in the morning. Bob home by seven most evenings. Sunday dinners with Ruthanne.

From a certain distance, the life looked exactly as it had.

But it wasn't.

Bob spent the next several years in the project of earning something back that he couldn't quite name and couldn't fully reach. He was home more. He asked more questions. He was more careful in the hundred small ways that marriage is made of small ways, and she let him try—not cruelly, not in the way of someone keeping score, but in the honest way of someone who has accepted a certain version of things and is not going to pretend otherwise. The pretending had never been her.

She was a good wife to him in the ways she had agreed to be. Loyal. Faithful in the literal sense. Present at his professional events, gracious with his colleagues, interested in his work without performing the interest. She kept their household. She raised their children.

She just didn't wear the ring.

And everyone who knew them, and knew what the ring meant, understood what its absence said. They didn't say it back. They just knew.

She talked with her mother about it once. Only once, and only because Ruthanne asked directly, which was rare. The Essen women were not a family that asked directly about each other's private pain, because they understood that private pain was private for a reason.

It was a winter Sunday, two years after Bob had stepped out for something. The children were elsewhere. The two of them were in the kitchen with the dishes, and the winter light was thin and gray through the east-facing window, the garden outside bare.

Ruthanne said, "Are you all right? Not the way you answer when someone asks. The actual answer."

Honey dried her hands on the dish towel. She considered the question the way she considered most things: without rushing and without reaching for the easy answer.

"I'm all right," she said finally. "It's not the marriage I thought I was in. But I chose it. And I chose to stay in it. And I'm not going to spend the rest of my life feeling sorry for myself about either of those choices."

Ruthanne was quiet for a moment. Then: "That sounds like your father."

"Good."

"Your father also said once that not feeling sorry for yourself is different from not having anything to feel sorry about."

Honey looked at her mother. Ruthanne looked back with those eyes that had seen everything that had happened in this family and had kept honest track of most of it.

"I know the difference," Honey said.

"I know you do, sweetheart." Ruthanne took the dish towel from her and hung it precisely on the oven handle. "I just want you to know that you're allowed to have both. You're allowed to be the person who chose and stayed and the person who lost something. Those don't cancel each other out."

Honey nodded. She didn't trust herself, in that moment, to say anything more.

The dishes were done. They went back to the living room. The Sunday went on the way Sundays do, ordinary and specific, full of small things.

But she carried her mother's words with her, not as comfort, but as permission. Permission to hold both things at once, without needing one to win. The loss was real. The choice was real too. Both were true, and she was allowed to know it.

Chapter 7: What She Held

The children grew up.

This sounds simple, but it isn't. Growing up doesn't move smoothly from one stage to the next. It happens in fits and starts, with setbacks and surprises. Seeing it up close, when you're the one guiding it through the hardest parts, is nothing like watching from afar.

Carol was the first to leave home, and no one was surprised. She had her mother's decisiveness and her father's easy way with people, and together these made her move through life with a confidence Honey both recognized and quietly admired, even as she wished she'd found it herself. Carol went to college in Indiana, the first of the children to do so, which meant more to Honey than she ever said. She came home on breaks with stories from her classes, a boyfriend who lasted two semesters and then didn't, and later, a girlfriend she brought home at Christmas her senior year. Carol had told her parents about the girlfriend a month before, over the phone. Her father handled it better than Honey expected, but not as well as she'd hoped. Honey responded by asking about the girlfriend—her name, her work, what Carol loved about her—because that was what mattered most.

Carol's girlfriend became Carol's wife in 1998, a civil ceremony in another state because the alternatives were limited that year. Honey attended and stood in the second row with Bob beside her and watched her daughter marry a woman named Diane who looked at Carol with a steadiness and warmth that Honey recognized, and she thought: good. This is exactly right. She shook Diane's hand afterward and said, "I'm very glad to meet you properly," and meant it completely.

James was more difficult. He had been a challenge since he was thirteen, and he didn't become easier in the usual ways. Instead, things improved in sudden, uneven steps, like rough ground that finally smooths out if you keep going. He went to college, dropped out after a year and a half, worked at jobs that were fine but not quite right, then went back and finished. He had a six-year relationship with a woman named Karen, which ended in a way that made Honey hold back her true thoughts. She believed Karen had always tried to manage James instead of loving him, and that effort wore them both out. Honey kept this to herself until James, at thirty-two, said it first. She agreed, and when he asked why she hadn't told him, she said, "Because you needed to arrive at it yourself."

He met Diane, a different Diane by coincidence, which sometimes led to confusion at family gatherings. She worked in construction management and looked at James the way Honey had always hoped someone would: with clear eyes, real affection, and the steady patience of someone who had decided he was worth it and didn't doubt that choice.

Thomas was the one she worried about least and the one who called most often. He was forty years old and still called his mother every Sunday, which he had been doing since he left home at eighteen, and not out of obligation—out of actual desire to talk, which was the kind of thing that struck Honey on quiet Sunday evenings when the call was done as one of the great unremarked gifts of her life. That her youngest child, the quiet one, had grown up to be someone who simply wanted to tell her about his week.

Ruthanne died in 1989.

She died in her sleep at the house on Clement Avenue, in the bed she had shared with Harold for twenty years and then slept in alone for twenty-seven more. She was seventy. Through all those years, she stayed exactly who she had always been: interested, patient, generous with her attention, and quietly content with simple pleasures. The heart that failed Harold at fifty-one lasted longer in her, and she made good use of those extra years.

Dennis called Honey at five in the morning. She listened, said she'd be right there, and dressed in the dark without fully waking Bob, who reached for her arm as she stood and squeezed it once and let her go.

She drove through empty streets in the early morning darkness. The city was still asleep, and the traffic lights changed for no one. She didn't have to think about the way to Clement Avenue; she had been driving that route for twenty years.

She let herself in with her key and went up the stairs and into her mother's room and stood in the doorway.

The stillness of a body that has stopped is different from sleep in a way you cannot describe to someone who hasn't seen it, but you recognize it immediately and with certainty when you have. It is a stillness that has weight. It is absence made visible. Honey stood in the doorway and looked at her mother and understood completely and immediately and without requiring any further information.

She went to the chair by the window, the one her mother always used for reading, with its armrest worn down from years of use, and sat down. In the early morning darkness, she thought about her mother—what it meant to have had her, and what it meant to lose her now. She wasn't exactly praying, or even actively grieving yet. She was just sitting where her mother had been, in the quiet that comes at the end of something, trying to understand it fully before the day's demands began.

She was fifty years old.

She remembered a little girl in a park on Delmar Street, watching her mother push a stroller. She remembered curtains always clean and a kitchen table always set at six. She remembered a woman sitting at that table, hands flat on the surface, testing its strength the night the police arrived.

She thought about tomatoes. About how well her mother's garden had done this year, and how much Ruthanne had enjoyed talking about it.

She didn't cry until Dennis arrived, came through the door, crossed the room, and put his arms around her from behind. Older brothers can do this, once they've learned it's allowed. She cried against his shoulder, fully and briefly, without apology, just as she always did when she let herself cry. Then she stopped, and together they got on with what needed to be done, because that was all there was.

She was the matriarch now in a way that was no longer shared with anyone. Ruthanne had been, even in her last years, the person at the top of the family—the generation above, the original, the one whose loss would define a before and after. Now that position passed to Honey, not formally, not with any discussion, but the way these things pass: because she was the oldest, and because she had always been the one they called, and because the family understood—even if they'd never said it—that she was the center of the wheel.

She was good at it. She remained good at it into her sixties, seventies, and partway into her eighties, and the goodness of it—the reliability of her, the constancy—was so complete and so consistent that it had become, to the people who depended on it, invisible. Not invisible to them as individuals; they each knew she was there. They each knew she was the one who called on birthdays and who showed up in the difficult weeks and who held the full picture. But the cost of it was invisible. The effort was invisible. The weight she had been carrying since she was twelve years old on a porch step had been carried so long and so smoothly that it had stopped appearing, in anyone's accounting, as weight.

She was the one they called. The one who showed up. The one who knew what to do about the hospital, the school, the landlord, the legal problems that needed a steady hand, and the family arguments that needed careful attention.

Through it all, she also had a rich inner life that she mostly kept to herself—not out of secrecy, but because she believed the person who holds things together can't seem like someone who might let go. She read widely, from history to gardening to novels that made her laugh out loud when she was alone. She shared her sharp opinions on politics and science with people she trusted. Her humor was dry and subtle, sometimes only landing a moment after she spoke.

She gardened with real care, giving it the same focus she brought to everything else. She studied what each plant needed, paid attention to the soil and the light, and made changes as needed. The garden behind the house on Clement Road wasn't just for show. It was a real project.

Bob knew she was funny. Whatever else the years had made of their marriage—and the years had made many things, some of them difficult and some of them genuinely, unexpectedly good—he had kept paying attention to her in the way he'd described at Linda's wedding, forty years before. He knew who she was. He'd been watching long enough to know.

He just didn't always act like it. He loved her in the ways he was capable of loving, which were real ways, and fell short in others in the ways he was capable of falling short, which were also real. She had learned to hold this without bitterness—not always easily, not always without effort, but honestly. The marriage was what it was. She had made it what she could.

She was seventy-three when she could no longer work in the garden as easily as she had at sixty. Her right knee had bothered her for years, and she finally had it replaced. She was managing, but that was the key word, and she was honest with herself about it, just as she was about most things. She knew that lying to yourself was the costliest mistake.

She was seventy-six when Carol was diagnosed with breast cancer. For eight months, she drove three hours every weekend to sit in waiting rooms, bring food, and simply be there, because sometimes presence is the only thing you can offer. Carol recovered. The cancer didn't come back, and Honey felt a gratitude so deep she couldn't name it. She never let herself expect it, and she never spoke of the fear she'd carried for those eight months, because it hadn't come true, and words were for things that had.

She was seventy-eight when the cough started.

At first, it wasn't alarming. It was just a winter cough, a stubborn one that lingered. She had never been the type to rush to the doctor for every small problem—partly out of practicality, and partly because she knew she often put her own health last. She understood this habit, even if she knew it wasn't always wise.

By spring the cough had changed. Not loudly—just differently. By summer she had the particular private knowledge of a body trying to tell you something, and she made the appointment and she went to it alone, because she saw no reason to alarm anyone before there was something specific to be alarmed about.

Dr. Anand was a woman in her forties with a calm that Honey recognized immediately—the calm that comes from having delivered difficult news many times and having learned that the news itself is not the most important thing you deliver. How you say it is. She sat across from Honey and told her what the scans showed, directly and without decoration.

Metastatic lung cancer.

Honey asked the questions she needed to ask. She wrote the answers in the small notebook she had carried in her purse for thirty years—the size and kind that fit in her palm, that she'd used for grocery lists and appointments and phone numbers and the occasional note to herself that she needed to remember. She wrote down the words the doctor used and the numbers and the options.

She thanked Dr. Anand and shook her hand and walked out through the waiting room and down the corridor and through the lobby and out into the parking lot.

The afternoon was ordinary. The blue sky faded toward evening. Other people's cars sat in neat rows. The world continued on, completely unaware of what had just happened inside the building.

She sat in her car and looked at the parking lot for about ten minutes. She didn't cry. She just looked, letting the news settle into the bigger picture of her life, as she always did—by sitting with it, not rushing, and trusting that clarity would come if she gave it time.

Then she started the car and drove home to tell Bob.

Chapter 8: The Last Good Year

Bob cried when she told him. He sat down hard in the kitchen chair, the same one where he'd sat across from her thirty-some years ago with an untouched scotch. His face did what it sometimes did when he was overtaken by something: it collapsed briefly, the structure of it simply giving way, before he pulled it back together. He was a man who'd spent his professional life managing how he appeared in rooms, and the collapse was visible only because she knew what to look for. She had been reading his face for fifty years.

He cried and she sat across from him and told him what she knew in the clear, orderly way she told things, and when she was done he reached across the table and took her hand in both of his.

She let him hold it. She looked at his hands on hers, large and still, the knuckles thickened with age. The wedding ring he'd worn all these years fit differently now that his fingers had changed shape over the decades. She thought about how well she knew this hand. How many times she had seen it reach for her, push papers across a desk, plant tulip bulbs in the wrong spot while she watched from the kitchen window. The word 'knew' felt too small for the particular weight of sharing a life with someone.

She thought about this seriously, which was the only way she thought about things. "I need you to let me tell the children in my own way and my own time. I need you not to fall apart where I can see it. And I need," she said, "for the garden to be dealt with before the frost. I started it and I want it finished."

He looked at her. A small, complicated expression moved across his face.

"The garden," he said.

"There are tulip bulbs that haven't been planted. The purple ones, in the bag by the back door. They'll be no good if they sit through a freeze."

He closed his eyes briefly. "All right," he said. "All right."

He planted the bulbs the following weekend, on a gray Saturday when the air had the first real bite of October in it. She watched from the kitchen window with a cup of tea, her hands around the mug the way they had always wrapped around warm things, tracking him as he moved through the garden with the printout she'd made of the planting diagram. He got several things wrong. She tapped on the glass when he did, until he looked up, and she gestured corrections with her hand: a little left, deeper, no, not there. He adjusted without complaint, without the look some men get when corrected at physical tasks. He just moved the bulbs where she indicated and kept going.

He didn't get it exactly right even with the corrections. But he was trying, which was what she'd asked for, and she watched him bend over the bed in the October cold with something she recognized as tenderness. Not the kind she'd had at the beginning. The kind that comes after.

She told each child separately. This took three days and a good deal of careful scheduling, which she handled with the organizational precision of someone who had been managing complex logistics since she was seventeen and had never fully stopped.

Carol came over on a Tuesday afternoon and Honey told her over coffee at the kitchen table. Carol listened the way she always had to difficult things, very still, her face controlled, the emotion visible only around the eyes, in the slight tightening of the muscles there. She had her mother's way of receiving hard information: without flinching, without making it immediately about her own feelings, without requiring the person delivering it to also manage her response. When Honey finished, Carol set her coffee cup down precisely in the center of the saucer and said, "What do the doctors say about the timeline?"

"Honest estimates are difficult with this. Possibly a year. Possibly longer with treatment. Possibly less."

Carol nodded slowly, absorbing this the way a building absorbs a tremor, invisibly, through the structure. "What do you want the next year to look like?"

Honey had not expected the question to arrive so directly, and she felt a wave of something she hadn't been prepared for, not grief exactly, but a kind of unexpected gratitude. Here was her daughter, asking what she wanted. Not what the family needed. Not what would be manageable for everyone. What she, Honey, wanted.

She sat with it for a moment. "I want to see Thomas in the spring when the garden is coming in. I want to have Christmas at my house this year, with everyone here. And I want..." She paused, looking at her hands on the table. "I want to not be treated like I'm already gone. I'm still here and I intend to act like it for as long as I can."

Carol reached across the table and put her hand over her mother's. She said, "I can promise all of that." And she meant it in the way Carol meant things—not as reassurance but as a commitment, which was different.

She kept all three promises.

James arrived on Thursday evening and sat in the living room with his hands on his knees, the way he'd sat since he was thirteen, braced for something, as if life were a thing that came at you and the best you could do was absorb the impact. She sat across from him and told him, and his face went through changes. He was not as controlled as Carol, had never been, and she watched the emotions cross him without trying to manage them, trusting that he'd find his way back to level, which he always did eventually.

"I should have called more," he said.

"You called enough."

"No." He stopped, looked at his hands. Looked up. "There was always going to be more time. I kept thinking there was more time."

"James." She waited until he looked at her directly. "There is still time. That's what I'm telling you. Right now, there is still time, and I don't want to spend it watching you feel guilty about the past when we could be here together in the present. Do you understand what I'm asking?"

He understood. He didn't fully believe it yet. He'd always had to come to things through the guilt first before he could get to the other side of it, but he nodded and she accepted the nod.

Thomas she told last, on a Saturday, and he stayed the night. They talked until after midnight in the kitchen with the lights low, which they had never done before, and she told him things she'd told no one else: about Harold, about the coffee shop on Brentwood, about the regular kind of happy, about what she'd given up and what she'd chosen and how she felt about the choosing from this distance. Thomas sat across from her and listened in the particular way he'd always listened, completely, without interruption, without preparing his response while she was still talking.

When she was done he said, "You've been providing the regular kind of happy for everyone else your whole life."

"Yes," she said.

"That's not quite the same as having it."

She looked at him for a moment. "No. It isn't. But it's not nothing, either. The two things aren't as separate as they sound."

He accepted this, because he was the child most like her and he understood what she meant.

The year was harder than she'd let the doctors predict and better than she'd feared. This, she was learning, was the way of things. The reality of living was almost never as simply terrible as the imagined version.

She was tired in ways that were new to her. Not the fatigue of a long week or a difficult month, but something with more permanence to it, something that lived in the body at a different depth and didn't lift with sleep the way ordinary tiredness did. She recalibrated constantly. She was the one who decided what she could still do and what she couldn't, and she made these decisions without self-pity and without pretending, which was the only way she knew how to make decisions.

Bob stayed home more. This was not something she asked for but something he decided quietly and put into place without saying anything. He reduced his hours at the firm he'd made partner at years ago, spent fewer evenings out, and brought a different quality of presence to the house. She noticed it the way she noticed most things: completely, and without making a point of noticing. He brought her tea without being asked. He sat with her in the evenings when the fatigue was worst, putting on the British comedies she'd always liked, which he'd never shared and still didn't quite understand, and sitting beside her on the couch with his phone in his pocket rather than in his hand.

One evening she said to him, "You should have done this earlier."

He looked at her. "I know."

"I'm not saying it to cause pain. I'm saying it because it's true, and we're past the point of not saying true things."

"I know," he said again. The words were simple but they carried something. He put his arm around her, carefully, in the way he'd learned over this last year to hold her, like something that mattered, like something he understood might not always be there to hold.

She let herself lean into it. Not because everything was resolved between them, because it wasn't, and not because the past had been rewritten, because it hadn't. But because she was nearly eighty years old and she was tired and his shoulder was there and she had long since stopped confusing practicality with capitulation.

Carol kept her word about Christmas. They all came: the three children and their spouses, the grandchildren, and the two small great-grandchildren who had arrived in the last few years and who moved through the world with the absolute confidence of people who have never yet been told they take up too much space.

The house was full in the way family houses are when everyone arrives at once: noisily, imperfectly, with too much food on the counter and not enough chairs at the table and someone always standing in the kitchen doorway asking where the serving spoons were kept. Honey directed the kitchen from her chair at the table because standing for long stretches had become difficult, and she gave instructions with the efficiency of someone who had run this operation for fifty years and knew every variable.

Carol had reconfigured the seating at the table without saying anything about it, and Honey found herself at the head. She looked down the length of it at all of them talking and passing dishes and arguing pleasantly about something on the television in the next room, and she held what she was seeing with both hands, the way she had always held the things that mattered most.

James caught her eye from halfway down the table and raised his glass slightly. She inclined her head. Thomas, beside her, put his hand briefly over hers on the armrest.

The two great-grandchildren were in the corner making a mess with crackers, and someone had given them a bowl of grapes they were redistributing across the floor, and it was loud and imperfect and entirely real.

She looked at all of it and understood, with a completeness that surprised her even now, that this was what it had been for. Not the sacrifice. Not the cost. Not the giving up of the senior year and the graduation and the years of Fridays and the ring she'd taken off and never put back. The thing itself. This specific, imperfect, abundant family that would not have held together without her—that she had made, along with everyone else in this room, with her hands, every day, for sixty years.

She didn't say any of this. She just held it, the way she had always held the things that mattered, quietly, without calling attention to the act of holding, and she let the moment be exactly what it was.

Chapter 9: What She Left

She died in April.

It wasn't the cold, gray April that sometimes clings to winter. This April was different. It brought a gentle warmth, with light arriving earlier each morning and lasting longer each evening. The tulip bulbs Bob planted in the fall were already pushing up through the soil, showing the steady promise of things that have been cared for and are ready to grow.

She had been in hospice care for three weeks. The hospice nurses came and went quietly, which she appreciated. It wasn't the forced quiet of people trying to make things better, but the real quiet of those who knew this work was best done without fuss. She liked them. She had always liked people who were honest in what they did, even if not always in what they said, and the nurses were like that. They did their work efficiently and without drama, treating her with a respect she hadn't always received when she was healthy and easy to ignore.

She told Thomas during one of his visits that the male nurse, David, reminded her a little of her father. David had a way of being present in a room without taking up too much space. Thomas kept this to himself, because he was the one who knew when to hold onto things quietly.

Carol was there every day. She drove in from forty minutes away each morning and stayed until evening, taking care of what needed to be done. She coordinated with the nurses, managed prescriptions, and answered the phone so Bob didn't have to. She did all of this with a quiet competence she'd learned from her mother—efficiently, without drawing attention to herself, and in a way that left room for more than just the practical tasks.

James drove in from two states away at the start and stayed. He slept in his old room, now a guest room, but the morning light still reminded him of his childhood. He sat with her when Carol needed a break, and he was better at sitting still than ever before. This year had finally given James a reason to slow down and be present, something he had always needed but often avoided.

Thomas came every evening after work, and he and Honey had fallen into the habit of the late afternoon hour—he in the chair by the window, she propped against her pillows—talking or not talking according to what the hour required. Some evenings they talked about specific things: the garden, the family, a book she'd been reading in smaller increments as her attention shortened. Other evenings they sat in the kind of silence that is itself a form of presence, the kind you can only have with someone you know well enough not to fill.

Bob was there all the time.

He slept in the chair in the corner, taking turns with Carol. It wasn't that Honey needed someone there all the time, but he couldn't bring himself to be anywhere else. Over the past year, she had watched him come to terms with the reality of her, the fact that she would not always be there. He had known this in his mind for years, but now he was feeling it in a deeper way. There was something both right and a little too late about it, and she had accepted that. It wasn't a cheerful acceptance, but the kind that comes from sitting with something long enough to understand it instead of trying to change it.

She had been in her marriage for fifty-three years. She had been in it through things that would have ended other people's marriages, and through things that had quietly sustained it, and through decades of ordinary life that were neither devastating nor transcendent but simply continuous. She had been in it faithfully and without performing that faithfulness, and she had arrived at the end of it knowing that the love between them was real, the relationship was imperfect, and both of those things were true at the same time and always had been.

In other words, she had ended up exactly where she had always been. It was an ordinary kind of truth.

She wanted to see the garden before she couldn't anymore. It was a Thursday morning, ten days before she died, and she still had a little time when being outside was possible with help. The April light came through the curtains, reminding her that the world outside was still going on as usual.

Bob brought the wheelchair. He didn't ask if she needed it; by now, he knew the difference between asking and doing. He simply had it ready when she said she wanted to go out. He helped her from the bed into the chair with the careful skill of someone who had watched the nurses closely and paid attention because it mattered to him.

He pushed her out through the sliding door to the garden.

The morning was cool, so she had a blanket across her lap. The tulips had come up and bloomed: red, yellow, and the deep purple he had added along the east edge of the bed, a row he had extended in the years after she died. She looked at them for a long time. She wasn't cataloguing or judging, just seeing what was there.

The garden wasn't perfect. It was a real garden, not a magazine garden, with bare patches and overgrown sections and the corner along the fence that had never quite succeeded no matter what she'd put there. But it was alive and it was blooming and the colors were exactly what she'd wanted when she'd pointed at the bulb catalog two falls ago and said: those. The purple ones. She had been thinking about next spring even then, which was the kind of thinking she'd always done.

"They came up," she said.

Bob was standing behind the chair. "They did."

"The purple ones were a guess. I wasn't certain they'd work with the others. The colors can fight if you're not careful."

"They don't fight," he said.

She looked at the flower bed for another moment. Then she placed her hand over the wheelchair armrest, and he took it—not reaching, just accepting—and held it the way you hold something you have held for fifty years and finally understand the weight of it. The light moved across the beds in the slow way of spring mornings, and a bird in the neighbor's maple was going through its full repertoire without conserving itself at all, giving everything it had to the April air. She listened to it and thought about nothing in particular, which was a thing she had rarely permitted herself and which she was learning, at the very end, to do.

When she was ready, Bob took the handles of the chair and pushed her back through the sliding door into the warmth of the house. In those few steps, she felt the weight of all their years together—the good and the complicated—and she thought: this is the full sum of a life. Not simple. Not tidy. But complete.

She asked them all to come on a Sunday.

They came. They filled the bedroom and spilled into the hallway, and there were grandchildren who had driven overnight and a great-grandchild asleep in a carrier and the room held all of them with a warmth that had nothing to do with the thermostat. She was tired in the way she was always tired now, the tiredness that had a direction to it, but she was awake and present and she looked at each person in the room with the attentiveness that had been her signature since childhood.

She said what she needed to say. There were no long speeches; she was never someone who talked much about her feelings, and that didn't change at the end. Authenticity doesn't fade at the end. It grows stronger.

To Carol she said: "You kept every promise you ever made me. I want you to know that I know that."

To James she said: "You became the man I always believed you were. It just took you longer to introduce yourself to him. I'm proud of you."

To Thomas she said: "You call your mother every Sunday. Don't stop that. Whoever needs it next will need it just as much."

To Bob she said, with all of them listening and not caring that they were listening: "You loved me. I want you to know that I know that. It wasn't always what I needed. But it was real, and real is what counts in the end."

He couldn't answer. His face changed in the way it always did when his emotions broke through.

She held his gaze steadily. "Keep the garden," she said. "The purple ones will come back in the spring."

He nodded. She let herself be surrounded by the people in the room. She stopped managing and simply allowed herself to be close to them, something she had rarely done. It turned out to be enough—more than enough. It was everything.

She died on a Thursday morning at six forty-two, in the bed she had shared with Bob for decades. The April light came through the window just as she liked it: low, direct, and simple.

Carol and Bob were in the room. Thomas arrived fourteen minutes later, having driven ninety miles in the dark when the call came, and he sat in the chair by the window for a long time afterward. The chair still held the shape of where he'd been sitting all these evenings, which was a comfort to him in the way that small physical facts are comforting when larger ones are too large to hold.

James came by noon. He stood in the doorway and looked at the bed for a long moment and then said, to no one in particular and to all of them at once: "She made this family. She just made it."

No one disagreed. There was nothing to add.

The service was exactly what she'd asked for—nothing she wouldn't have recognized as herself. The choir at the brick church on Clement and Vine sang, different voices from the ones she'd heard as a child but the same sound somehow, because choirs outlast their members the way families outlast their individuals. People came who hadn't seen her in years and stood outside afterward in the spring air and told stories. Not eulogies—stories. The specific, irreplaceable kind that arrive when people feel the loss of someone who was genuinely present in their lives: what she had said, how she had helped, the phone calls, the showing up, the particular quality of attention she'd given to everyone she'd loved.

Thomas kept count of the stories without meaning to. He lost count somewhere around forty.

Bob held her ashes in the box they had chosen with care. He held it the way he had held her hand in the garden, with the careful, full attention of someone who had finally, completely understood what he was holding.

He carried her home.

Chapter 10: The Stone

Bob Tennyson died five years after his wife.

He was eighty-seven, and for those five years he carried a quiet, steady grief that his children saw but didn't always know how to handle. He took care of the garden with the focus of someone following clear instructions. He went to the church on Clement and Vine, always sitting in the third pew on the left—their spot for forty years. He sat in the whole pew instead of moving to the center, something Carol noticed every time she joined him, though she never mentioned it.

He always showed up on time for the dinners his children planned, seeing his punctuality as a way to say thank you. He sat with them, ate their food, and joined their conversations about the grandchildren, the news, changes in the neighborhood, and the garden. Everyone agreed he seemed to be doing fine. He had always seemed fine on the outside. She had understood this about him, and now the children were starting to see it too.

He kept her ashes on the mantel in the living room, in a box they had chosen carefully. Sometimes, when he was alone, he talked to her. After sharing a life for so long, it was hard to stop talking just because she was gone. He told her about the garden. He told her the purple tulips had come back the second year and that he had planted more, making the row along the fence longer. She probably would have pointed out a better spot from the kitchen window, tapping on the glass the way she did when words were too much.

He told her he was sorry. He said it more than once, quietly, like someone who finally faces the truth and finds it hard. He told her she had deserved better in some ways, and he meant it. She wasn't there to tell him she already knew and had made peace with it long ago. Maybe that was the only mercy—that she didn't have to hear it all again.

He took care of his affairs carefully during those five years. He had always been good at handling the details—wills, accounts, and plans for what came next. He managed everything with the same careful attention he had used in his work, because being thorough was what he did best, even in old age.

He arranged, among other things, his gravestone.

Thomas found out about the gravestone by accident.

He had been going through his father's papers with Carol—the archaeology of a person's life, which is what death reduces everything to eventually: folders and envelopes and documents that meant a great deal to someone and now require sorting by people who are still figuring out their own grief in the middle of the sorting—when he found the printout from the monument company. A confirmation of the order. The text that had been reviewed and approved and sent back with a signature.

He picked it up and read it because it was there and he was reading everything that was there.

He read it twice. Then he set it on the dining room table and looked at it for a moment before Carol came over and read it herself.

The stone was large. The printout listed its size—a big slab of granite picked to last. At the top was Robert Allen Tennyson. Underneath were the dates. Then came the organizations: the Rotary Club, where he had been a member for thirty-one years and president for two, the advertising industry association where he was on the board, the civic group he joined in his fifties and led for ten years, and the golf club.

All of this took up most of the face of the stone.

At the very bottom, below the memberships, below the offices held, below the decades of civic engagement, in letters smaller than everything above them, was a single line.

Together forever with Honey

Not: *Beloved wife Veronica Essen Tennyson*

Not her name. Not her dates. Not the year she was born or the year she died or any of the specific, irreplaceable facts of her existence on this earth.

Just the word the woman at the park had said on a Saturday morning in 1950, looking at a platinum-haired baby in a stroller.

Honey.

Thomas sat with the printout for a long time after Carol went into the kitchen.

He sat with it the way his mother used to—facing things head-on, not looking away, trying to understand what he was really seeing before deciding what to do. He wanted to be fair. He wanted to understand what his father meant, because intention mattered, and because Bob had loved his mother as best he could—genuinely, imperfectly, and often without seeing the gap between what he felt and what he showed.

Bob had loved her. Thomas knew this with certainty. He had watched it from childhood, had seen his father's face when she walked into a room, had noticed the way Bob tracked her in a crowd without appearing to, the way his attention always found her even when he was in conversation with someone else. That love was real. It had always been real.

Bob had also set up a gravestone that listed four organizations and two board roles before mentioning the woman he had been married to for fifty-three years. And even then, he didn't use her real name—not the full, legal name that was hers alone—but a childhood nickname.

It was the name everyone used, from the woman in the park to the cashier at the grocery store where she shopped for forty years. He thought about her pressing shirts at seventeen in the back of a dry cleaner's she had already outgrown. He thought about Hendricks Department Store and the floor manager who looked past the piece of paper and saw what she could do. He thought about the ring on the table between his parents, placed without drama, without performance, because she was not a woman who performed.

He thought about her at the head of the Christmas table, looking down the length of it at all of them, the grandchildren and the great-grandchildren and the noise and the mess and the food, and the expression on her face that he had stored away without a word for it until now.

The word was home. She had looked at the thing she had built and she had known it for home.

He thought about forty years of Sunday phone calls that now had nowhere to go. He would pick up his phone on Sunday evenings out of habit, then set it down again. The silence where her voice used to be wasn't something you got used to. You just learned to carry it in a new way over time.

He didn't tell Carol what he felt about the stone. He didn't tell James, who had a temper that was better than it had been in his youth but still had edges when the thing that provoked it was large enough. He said nothing to the grandchildren.

He kept it to himself, the way his mother had done with most things—holding it quietly, letting it settle in the part of him where he kept what couldn't be changed and what didn't need to be said out loud to be real.

He tried to be fair. He understood that Bob had not meant it as an erasure. The stone had been arranged by a man in his eighties, grieving, who had loved his wife and who had also, throughout their entire married life, arranged the world in a way that put himself at the center of it—not cruelly, not with intent, but with the natural, unexamined confidence of a man of his generation who had never been asked to examine it. The stone was not malice. The stone was just Bob—the same Bob who had waited six years to marry her and had betrayed her and had planted tulip bulbs mostly right and had held her hand in the garden—the same, consistent, imperfect Bob, expressing himself in granite the way he had expressed himself in life.

This didn't make it right.

Thomas folded the printout, put it in his jacket pocket, and took it home. He placed it in his desk drawer. For months, he would open the drawer, look at it, and close it again, not sure what to do with his feelings or if anything needed to be done at all.

What he kept thinking about wasn't the stone itself, but what it said about who gets remembered, and how, and by whom. He had seen his mother run the family for sixty years—so completely and so much a part of daily life that everyone stopped seeing it as work and started seeing it as just the way things were. She was always there. She held everything up, like a foundation under a house—present, strong, and unseen until something changed and you realized what had been holding the weight all along.

The gravestone proved what she had likely known all her life: the invisible work, no matter how important, doesn't get carved into stone. The work that keeps everything together only shows up in the record if someone chooses to put it there. In the end, Bob hadn't chosen to. Not because he wanted to diminish her, but because he never really saw how much she carried, even after all those years.

The tulips came back the spring after Bob's funeral.

Thomas went to the house. Carol had kept it in the family for now, since none of them were ready to let go of the rooms that still held her scent and the garden she had tended for fifty years. He walked through the house slowly, taking his time, moving through a place that now felt empty. Then he stepped outside through the sliding door.

The beds were a little unruly, a season of maintenance deferred, but the tulips had come up exactly where Bob had planted them and she had directed him: red and yellow and the deep purple row along the fence that he had extended after she died, as if he had understood, at least in the garden, what needed to continue.

Thomas stood in the garden for a long time. The morning was the kind of April day that felt real—clear sky, warm sunlight, and the smell of freshly turned soil. A bird in the neighbor's tree sang loudly, probably just as it had every April, filling the morning with its song.

He thought about the stone in the cemetery where both his parents now rested together. His casket and her ashes were together, just as Bob had wanted. The granite listed all of Bob's names and titles, and at the bottom, in smaller letters, it read: *Together forever with Honey.*

He thought about a park on Delmar Street and a woman in a yellow blouse bending down to a stroller, searching for a word and finding it.

He thought about being ten, wearing a rented jacket at a family wedding, and dancing with his mother because she quietly asked him. He had never been able to say no to her, and he never wanted to.

He remembered his mother calling every Sunday evening, her voice always the same, interested in everything he said. She would remember what he told her and ask about it the next week—not as a trick, but because she truly wanted to know how things turned out.

He thought about what it meant that he now stood in her garden, in her spring light, saying her name out loud to the tulips she had planted and the gap in the air where she was not.

Veronica Essen Tennyson

He said her name to the garden, to the April morning, to no one in particular and to the unique, irreplaceable absence that was now everywhere and would stay with him for the rest of his life.

He said it the way you say something that should have been said louder and more often and carved into something that lasted.

Veronica.

Honey.

Here. Irreplaceable. Gone.

About the Author

P.A. Farrell writes accessible fiction that resonates with readers. Her work focuses on authentic human experiences and the quiet resilience of ordinary people facing extraordinary challenges. She is an accomplished flash fiction author whose compelling micro-narratives have captivated readers across the literary landscape. With over forty publications in prestigious online journals and literary magazines, Farrell has established herself as a master of the abbreviated form, crafting complete worlds and complex emotions within the constraints of brief word counts.

Her expertise in flash fiction extends beyond individual pieces to comprehensive collections, where she shows remarkable range and consistency in delivering powerful, bite-sized stories that linger long after the last sentence. Each collection showcases her ability to explore diverse themes, characters, and settings while maintaining the precision and impact that define exceptional flash fiction.

Farrell's work also resonates with readers who appreciate literature that delivers maximum emotional and intellectual impact in minimal space. Her stories often examine the pivotal moments that define the human experience, capturing the essence of larger truths through carefully chosen details and expertly crafted prose. The breadth of her publication history speaks both to her prolific output and the consistent quality that editors and readers expect from her work.

Through her continued contributions to the flash fiction genre, P.A. Farrell has become a trusted voice for readers seeking literature that respects their time while enriching their understanding of the human condition. Her collections offer the perfect opportunity to experience the full range of her storytelling abilities in a single, cohesive volume.

In her other life, P. A. Farrell is a clinical psychologist who has written several self-help books and continues to contribute to media outlets such as Medium.com and bluesky.com, where she posts articles on all aspects of healthcare, mental health, and a variety of other topics. Her Author's Page is here: https://tinyurl.com/4ewdunb8

Books by P. A. Farrell

Snowbound Hearts

The Secrets We Keep

The Secrets We Keep 2

Whispers Across the Sea

Love by the Latte

Echoes of Expectation—Waiting

Unexpected Short Tales of Surprise

A Special Request

If this book has touched your heart, sparked your curiosity, or simply entertained you along the way, I'd be incredibly grateful if you could take a moment to share your thoughts with a review on Amazon or wherever you discovered this book. Your words not only help other readers find books they'll love, but they also mean the world to authors like me who pour their hearts into every page. Thank you for being part of this journey, and for helping stories find their way to the readers who need them most. Her Author Page on Amazon: https://tinyurl.com/4ewdunb8

A Special Request

www.ingramcontent.com/pod-product-compliance
Lightning Source LLC
La Vergne TN
LVHW090616110826
845146LV00001B/419

* 9 7 9 8 9 9 3 7 3 9 6 7 0 *